Your Dog's
Wild Cousins

Also by Hope Ryden

YOUR DOG'S WILD COUSINS

photographs and text by Hope Ryden

Lodestar Books

Dutton   New York

Library of Congress Cataloging-in-Publications Data
Ryden, Hope
Your dog's wild cousins / photographs and text by Hope Ryden.
1st ed.   p.   cm   Includes index.
ISBN 0-525-67482-9
1. Canidae—Juvenile literature.   2. Dogs—Juvenile literature
[1. Canidae.   2. Wild dogs.]   I. Title
QL737.C22R94   1994
599.74'442—dc20
93-26855   CIP   AC

Published in the United States by Lodestar Books,
an affiliate of Dutton Children's Books,
a division of Penguin Books USA Inc.,
375 Hudson Street, New York, New York 10014
Published simultaneously in Canada
by McClelland & Stewart, Toronto
Editor: Virginia Buckley   Designer: Carolyn Boschi
Printed in Hong Kong
First Edition
1 3 5 7 9 10 8 6 4 2

for Zoe and Smiley, who found me,
and all the stray dogs like them
who are looking for a home

Acknowledgments

A number of the animals in this book were photographed in the wild. Some species, however, have become so endangered that it would be impractical to search for them in their shrinking habitats. The red wolf, for example, exists only in captive breeding programs and in one protected sanctuary. The South American maned wolf is in such decline that it, too, is being bred at the National Zoological Park in Front Royal, Virginia, for future release. The African wild dog is now thought to be the most endangered large carnivore in all of Africa, and several zoos are breeding it. The dhole of Asia, according to experts, can no longer survive outside of protected areas. And current knowledge of the bush dog has become limited to occasional sightings. The story goes on and on. As a result, I visited a number of sanctuaries that offer zones of protection for declining species, several zoos that are actively engaged in breeding programs, and one rehabilitation center, where ailing animals are restored to health and returned to the wild. In all of these places I was treated graciously, given up-to-date information, and invited to photograph rare or hard-to-find canids for this book.

I am indebted to the following: The Woodford Cedar Run Wildlife Refuge in Medford, New Jersey; the San Diego Zoo in California; the Burnet Park Zoo in Syracuse, New York; the National Zoo in Washington, D.C.; the National Zoological Park's Conservation and Research Center in Front Royal, Virginia; the Chicago Brookfield Zoo; the Philadelphia Zoo; the Van Saun Zoo in Paramus, New Jersey; the Beardsley Zoo in Bridgeport Connecticut; the Ross Park Zoo in Binghamton, New York; the Bronx Wildlife Conservation Park in New York; and the Healesville Wildlife Sanctuary in Australia.

CONTENTS

DOMESTIC DOG

Meet Zoe and Smiley. They are domestic dogs, meaning they live with human beings. Unlike their wild relatives, they do not have to hunt for food or create their own shelter. Nevertheless, they share many traits with their wild cousins, who do make their own living. Like the red fox, they have keen noses and are good at following scent trails. Like the coyote, they are clever and like to play. And like the gray wolf, they are loyal to their pack leader—who happens to be me!

The scientific name for the domestic dog is *Canis familiaris*. People have bred dogs to look many ways. Dogs may have long hair, short hair, or no hair at all. Some are giants; others are midgets. Some have stand-up ears; others have ears that hang down into their water dishes. Dogs can be black, brown, tan, white, orange, red, yellow, blue, or a combination of these colors. For that matter, two dogs can look so different that you may wonder how each knows the other is a dog. But they do. That's because they act alike.

For example, all dogs wag their tails when they are pleased and growl when they are angry. To show affection, they lick each other's muzzles (or your face, for that matter). This helps them make friends and avoid fights. Dogs developed these social skills long ago, when they lived in packs and hunted together. Today, your dog uses its tail, body, face, and voice to tell *you* how it feels.

Did you ever wonder how dogs came to live with us?

GRAY WOLF

Scientists tell us that the domestic dog is descended from the gray wolf. Some breeds, such as the Siberian husky and the German shepherd, certainly do look wolfish. Others, however, like the Pekingese or the Boston terrier, have been bred to look quite unlike their immediate ancestor. Yet, even these have been blessed with a wolf's nature. And it's a good thing!

The gray wolf is a sociable animal, at least with its fellow pack members. It regularly shows affection and goodwill, not just by licking and wagging its tail, but by joining in group

 The scientific name for the gray wolf is *Canis lupus*. Once, it was common everywhere in the Northern Hemisphere. Today, it has all but vanished from Asia, the Middle East, and Europe. In North America it holds its own only in Canada, Alaska, and Minnesota. Elsewhere, it is officially listed as endangered or extinct.

howls and presenting a friendly face. Such behavior strengthens the trust that exists among wolves, who need each other's help to surround and kill dangerous moose and caribou. A wolf is too large an animal to survive entirely on the small creatures it can catch on its own.

Of course, conflicts are bound to arise, even in a friendly wolf pack, but these are nearly always resolved peaceably. Whichever wolf has less status will automatically give way to the higher-ranking wolf. It does this by rolling onto its back in a submissive posture like the wolf pictured here. What's surprising is that the higher-ranking wolf does not bite the wolf that is down. Instead, it accepts the lower-ranking wolf's signal of defeat and backs off.

Actually, this behavior makes a lot of sense. Why would a wolf want to injure or kill one of its valuable hunting partners?

Is Smiley presenting a friendly face like his closest relative?

AUSTRALIAN DINGO

One way to understand how the wolf gave rise to the dog is to study the Australian dingo. This animal is a living example of early dog. To this day, its teeth remain more wolflike than doglike. Despite its name, however, the Australian dingo did not originate in Australia. It was brought to that continent by Stone Age people. Scientists have pieced together the story.

Many thousands of years ago, long before records were kept, some Asian wolves took to feeding on scraps, which they found scattered around human campsites. Mostly these wolves created no

trouble for the people and were ignored. Any that showed threatening behavior, however, were chased away or killed. As a result, only good-tempered animals remained, and they gave birth to easygoing offspring like themselves. As time passed, these scavengers took on a different appearance—less wolfish and more like a new species, which indeed they had become. A primitive form of dog had come into existence.

What happened next? Early dog grew friendlier and begged food scraps directly from the people. (That would make a hit with some folks!) Hunting tribes likely put some of these canids to work tracking animals. In short, a bond was formed between man and dog. One group of Asians even took their dogs along when they paddled across the Indian Ocean to Australia. On arrival, these primitive dogs reverted to the wild, and over the next five thousand years, they lived and bred in isolation. Not until the last century did modern man meet this living example of early dog.

Does your dog beg for food? Do you find this behavior appealing?

 The scientific name of the Australian dingo is *Canis familiaris dingo*. It is found only in Australia.

RED FOX

Have you ever read a story in which a sly red fox outwitted all the other animals? Such tales have grown out of people's real life experiences with this clever cousin of the dog. For when chased by hunters or set upon by a pack of hounds, this little canid knows how to confuse an enemy. Sometimes, it loses a pursuer by jumping back and forth across a stream. At other times, it runs atop a wall, where dogs won't find its strong scent. As a result, the red fox continues to thrive, even though it is everywhere chased and trapped by human beings for sport and fur.

Probably no animal has a better nose than the red fox. It sniffs out underground mice, digs them up, and eats them headfirst, as the fox in this picture is doing. It also uses scent to transmit messages. Special glands on its feet leave a smelly track wherever it walks, which warns other foxes not to trespass on its territory. Thus, red foxes space themselves apart and prevent their individual food supplies from being used up. Unfortunately, their foxy trails are easy for hound dogs to follow. This puts them at a terrible disadvantage.

Not all members of this species look the same, although most wear a thick red coat and black stockings. Some, however, are all black. A few pale yellow ones have one dark stripe down their back and another across their shoulders. A fox that is born with this pattern is called a cross fox, even though it is the same species as its red or black brothers and sisters.

Can your dog sniff out underground mice?

 The scientific name for the red fox is *Vulpes vulpes*. Red foxes are found throughout Asia, Europe, and the Middle East, and they occupy many parts of the United States and Canada as well.

DHOLE

The mountain-dwelling dhole is the champion long-distance jumper of the canid world. It perfected this skill during many ages of bounding from rock to rock in pursuit of prey. One dhole at the Moscow Zoo cleared all the walls and moats surrounding its pen in a single eighteen-foot-long leap!

Though dholes are fearsome hunters and have even been known to drive leopards from kills, there is no record of them ever attacking a human being. Certainly they are good-natured among themselves. Sometimes several families form an oversized pack, numbering as many as twenty-five animals. Unlike wolves, these packs do not engage in prehunt howls. When excited, they chatter and produce whistling noises that sound more like squabbling birds than rowdy canids.

A dhole looks much like a bushy-tailed, round-eared, domestic dog in a red coat. It differs from a domestic dog in several respects, however. For one thing, it possesses two fewer teeth. Also, a female

dhole has twice as many mammary glands as a female dog, which would enable her to nurse up to sixteen pups at a time. Since a dhole seldom gives birth to even half that number, this feature is something of a mystery. Perhaps the dhole no longer reproduces at the rate it once did, and that's too bad. For even though several females in a pack will whelp their litters in adjoining caves, the species is in decline. In every country where this beautiful wild cousin of the dog is found, it is listed as rare.

Does your dog make flying leaps?

 The scientific name for the dhole is *Cuon alpinus*. Though it enjoys a wide range, which includes the mountainous regions of China, Russia, India, and Southeast Asia, it is rare everywhere.

GRAY FOX

The gray fox is the only member of the canid family that can climb a tree. Though its claws are not as sharp as a cat's, they are long and connected to strong muscles, which enable it to grip bark. By hugging a trunk with its forelegs and boosting itself with its rear legs, it can vanish into a tree crown like some kind of oversized squirrel. Once there, it climbs into a hole and goes to sleep or jumps from branch to branch in pursuit of birds.

A gray fox does not dig its own den. Perhaps its tree-climbing claws are not well shaped for that purpose. Instead, it takes possession of some other animal's abandoned burrow. Or it may make do

 The scientific name for the gray fox is *Urocyon cinereoargenteus*. It lives in wooded areas throughout the United States, Mexico, and Central America and has recently spread into northern South America. Meanwhile, it has disappeared from Canada.

with a hollow log or stump. But wherever the gray fox does settle, it stays. Unlike other wild canids, this one occupies its den not just in spring when babies are born but all year round.

Like many of its cousins, the gray fox's babies remain with their mother for several months before setting off on their own. When conflicts arise, brothers and sisters settle their differences without biting one another. If one feels threatened by another, it simply opens its mouth wide and displays its teeth, like the animal pictured here, and the offender will back off. This is called gaping, and it serves the gray fox well. A species born with sharp teeth, which are needed to catch prey, must take care not to use these deadly weapons against its own kind or it risks becoming extinct. All your dog's cousins use facial expressions and body postures to help keep the peace.

Can your dog dig a den for itself?

COYOTE

If ever there was an adaptable animal, it is the coyote. This animal can live in a desert, forest, swamp, or even in the suburbs of a city! It eats rabbits, mice, birds, fruit, insects, garbage, and any already dead critter it finds. On occasion, it teams up with other coyotes to run down animals as large as deer. Usually the coyote hunts alone, however, for, unlike the wolf, it is small enough to survive on what it can catch by itself.

Of all your dog's wild cousins, the coyote may be the smartest. To locate food, this wily scavenger keeps an eye on the sky for ravens and vultures. It seems to understand that ravens and vultures fly in circles above a dead or dying animal. Coyotes also use their superb hearing to pinpoint the location of voles moving under the snowpack. And should a coyote spy a badger digging for ground squirrels, it will quickly post itself at one of the colony's many exit holes and catch any animal that tries to escape by that route.

Coyote pairs stay together for as long as they both live. When pups are born, the male brings food to the nursing mother, and when their babies are old enough to eat solid food, he provides for them, too. So do the pair's grown offspring, who were born the previous year. Throughout the day, these helpers return to the den and

upchuck mice for the new litter. Though such a meal sounds unappealing, partly digested mice make good puppy food.

Many Native American tribes greatly respected the clever coyote and invented wonderful stories about it. They called it Trickster.

Does your dog hear sounds that are inaudible to you?

 The coyote's scientific name is *Canis latrans*. Originally an animal of the North American West, it has recently extended its range to include many eastern states.

KIT FOX

One name for a baby fox is kit. This has led to some confusion, since that is also the name given to a particular *species* of fox. To complicate matters, the adults of this species are so tiny that they are sometimes mistaken for babies. A full-grown kit fox weighs only five pounds. That's smaller than the average house cat.

This dainty fox is a resident of the American desert and is well adapted for life in that hot, dry home. Lack of water is no problem. What moisture it needs it gets from a diet of rodents, lizards, insects, plants, and eggs. And kit foxes beat the heat by staying underground during most of the day. Not until late afternoon do they come out to hunt. At first, the bright desert light may cause an

animal to squint, like the fox pictured above. Soon, however, its eyes adjust to the harsh glare, and their round pupils shut down and become long slits, like those of a cat. Only a few members of the dog family have eye pupils that take this shape when exposed to light.

Kit foxes are social animals. Both parents provide food for their infant offspring, and the family remains together long after the babies are able to hunt for themselves. Some youngsters don't set off on their own until they are more than a year old. Mothers and adult daughters have even been known to give birth and raise litters in connected burrows. That must make life easier for them. When one goes off to mouse, the other kit sits.

When your dog's pupils contract in bright light, do they remain round or become slits?

 The scientific name for the kit fox is *Vulpes velox*. It lives in the American Southwest. A slight variation of *Vulpes velox*, commonly called the swift fox, is found in some of the Great Plains states. The kit fox and the swift fox are two races of the same species.

RED WOLF

A red wolf is not a gray wolf with a red tint to its coat; it is an entirely different species. Nor is a red wolf's fur always red. It can be black.

This handsome animal shares many traits with its two closest relatives, the gray wolf and the coyote. Like its big gray wolf cousin, it is capable of killing large animals. And, like its little coyote cousin, it is full of mischief. Unlike these two species, however, the red wolf has always been restricted to one kind of habitat. It is at home only in the southern part of the United States, where much of its living space has been taken over by human beings. This partly accounts for its near extinction.

Fortunately, in 1977, some dedicated people set out to save this species. First they captured fourteen red wolves to use as breeding stock. Their plan was to increase numbers to a safer level and then set some animals free. By 1988, eight zoos were cooperating in the project, and the known red wolf population stood at eighty-eight. That same year, a few wolves were released in a protected wildlife refuge in North Carolina. It was a time of great suspense. Many people doubted that zoo-raised animals could survive on their own. As it turned out, not all of them did. Some, however, managed to find

 The red wolf's scientific name is *Canis rufus*. Its range was always limited to the southern United States between Florida and Texas and northward to southern Indiana and Missouri. It is the most endangered of all your dog's wild cousins.

mates and raise pups in underground burrows—like the one the wolf above is standing in.

Since that time, more captive-bred red wolves have been turned loose in North Carolina, and the United States Fish and Wildlife Service hopes to find other safe places in which to set free still more of these beautiful native animals.

Does Zoe's friend Lina look like a red wolf?

MANED WOLF

The oddest cousin of your dog and mine is the maned wolf. Its shaggy coat is bright red, and its legs are longer than its body, making it look like an overgrown fox on stilts. It has a coarse black mane, like that of a horse, and a most peculiar way of trotting: It moves both legs on the same side of its body together, instead of alternating them. (Horses that trot this way are called pacers.) Lastly, the maned wolf isn't a wolf at all, but belongs in a category all its own. Early settlers in South America wrongly identified it.

Of course, traits that strike us as strange can serve an animal well. For example, the maned wolf's ridiculously long legs enable it to spot prey over the tall grasses that cover much of its habitat.

Actually, the maned wolf is not much of a hunter. Half of its diet consists of plant food and insects. Its favorite meal is a kind of wild potato that South Americans call wolf fruit. What small rodents it does eat can be caught without the help of hunting partners, so the maned wolf, unlike true wolves, has developed a solitary life style.

Although mates share the same territory, they mostly avoid each other, and the male takes no part in the rearing of the young. Nevertheless, his presence in the area is useful. By marking the habitat with strong scent, he warns away other maned wolves that might otherwise use up food needed by the mother and her pups.

In what order does your dog move its legs?

 The maned wolf's scientific name is *Chrysocyon brachyurus*. It lives on the savannas, or grasslands, of Brazil, Bolivia, and northern Argentina. It is extremely rare, and efforts are being made to breed it in captivity for future release.

19

BUSH DOG

At first glance, the South American bush dog looks more like an otter or a badger than a wild canid. Its legs appear too short for its body. Its middle two toe pads are fused—a peculiarity that may help it to swim, for the bush dog spends a good deal of time in water. In addition, it has six fewer teeth than your dog or mine. Finally, it doesn't sound like any other member of the canid kingdom. When excited, it produces piercing squeals and deafening cries.

Nevertheless, this terrier-sized animal is indeed a wild cousin of the dog and, judging by its fossil remains, an ancient one. As skilled a predator as the wolf, it is equally sociable. That's because the bush dog needs helpers to bring down animals many times its size and weight. It must also use clever ruses to outsmart such large prey. Sometimes, when pursuing a deer or a capybara—a hog-sized animal—part of the pack will split off and enter a river. There they swim about and wait for the rest of the pack to drive the prey animal into the water, where it can be quickly killed.

The South American bush dog is seldom seen, for its short legs

enable it to scoot about under dense vegetation and escape notice. But despite its ability to remain under cover, this pint-sized cousin of the dog is in decline. Much of its habitat has been converted into ranches and farms. And without suitable habitat, no animal, however clever and elusive, can survive.

Does your dog like to play in water?

 The bush dog's scientific name is *Speothos venaticus*. It is native to the northern countries of South America. It is listed as rare.

FENNEC

The North African fennec is the smallest of your dog's wild cousins. It is even smaller than the North American kit fox. Like the kit fox, however, its behavior and body have been shaped by life in the desert, where temperatures are extremely hot and water is scarce.

In such places, an ordinary dog would pant nonstop to cool itself down. A fennec cannot afford such luxury, for continuous panting creates thirst, and a fennec must get along with little or no water. As a result, it has come up with other ways to survive the heat. It sel-

dom ventures out of its burrow before sunset. It sports a pale yellow coat, which reflects rather than absorbs the sun's scorching rays. Its wooly undercoat insulates its body from the desert's high temperatures. Its footpads are covered with matted fur to protect them from the burning sands of the great Sahara Desert. Finally, its enormous ears act like radiators, causing the fennec to *lose* body heat to the air.

These enormous ears have other functions, too. They amplify the faint scurrying sounds made by rodents and insects and thus help this animal to hunt at night. They also communicate mood. Depending on their position, they can mean different things. For example, the laid-back ears of the fennec in the opposite picture warn, "Don't crowd me or I'll attack." Since fennecs sometimes live in small social groups, they need to use body language in order to get along with one another.

How do dogs cool down after playing too hard?

 The scientific name of the fennec is *Fennecus zerda*. It lives in a vast desert that covers most of North Africa.

BLACK-BACKED JACKAL

The black-backed jackal has the most distinctive markings of all your dog's wild cousins. It is tricolored. It wears a saddle of black, silver-tipped guard hairs across its back. Its chest and belly are white. The rest of its body is a rich orange. In addition, the black-backed jackal is well formed with bright black eyes. A breed of dog as handsome as this would certainly make a hit at a dog show. Nevertheless, the word *jackal* does not call to mind a beautiful animal. On the contrary. Because this word has been wrongly applied to describe a sneaky person, the jackal itself has acquired a bad name.

Actually, the jackal is so closely related to man's best friend, the dog, that the two can interbreed. Some scientists even suspect that certain breeds of dogs resulted from past crosses between these two species. In some respects, the jackal is even more admirable than the dog, for it remains loyal to its mate for life. What's more, jackal fathers, unlike dog fathers, take part in the care and feeding of their pups.

Jackals usually hunt alone or in pairs, but if small prey is scarce,

several will team up to bring down an antelope. Often an easier meal is provided by lions. When jackals spot a pride of lions feeding on a kill, they gather on the sidelines and wait with growing excitement and much yapping until the big cats have eaten their fill. Then they slip in and gobble up the scraps.

How does your dog feel about eating leftovers?

 The scientific name for the black-backed jackal is *Canis mesomelas*. It makes its home on the savannas and in the scrub forests of eastern and southern Africa.

BAT-EARED FOX

The bat-eared fox's face is so tiny that you have to wonder how it can hold so many teeth—forty-eight! That's six more than you will find in your dog's mouth. It's more than hyenas, bears, or tigers possess. If you exclude Australian marsupials, the only mammal that has more teeth than this pint-sized canid is the gigantic humpback whale.

You might expect an animal with such impressive teeth to be a fearsome hunter. Not so. Half of a bat-eared fox's diet consists of termites, which it crunches up by the mouthful. If termites are not available, it listens for beetles crawling in the grass—like the animal pictured here. Grubs, fruit, and carrion are also relished by this gentle resident of the African plains. Warm-blooded animals make up only 10 percent of what it eats.

Obviously, such a diet does not require the bat-eared fox to have hunting partners. Nevertheless, it often forages in groups. After devouring a nest of termites, several foxes may lie down and groom one another. They can't become too relaxed, however, for even though their brown coats serve to camouflage them in the grass, these little canids are at risk. The bat-eared fox is a favorite food of the leopard and is also eaten by wild dogs, jackals, and hawks.

Oddly enough, lions pose less of a threat to it. Sometimes the big cats even allow it a place on their kills. One naturalist tells of watching a lioness take a bat-eared fox between her front paws and wash it with her big tongue. The little fox, he said, did not seem at all alarmed. After its rough bath, it got to its feet, shook itself, and sauntered off. Maybe that lioness wasn't hungry.

Have you ever counted your dog's teeth?

 The scientific name of the bat-eared fox is *Otocyon megalotis*. It prefers open grasslands, but it also inhabits semideserts in eastern and southern Africa.

AFRICAN WILD DOG

Talk about being sociable! The African wild dog lives in packs that number as many as forty animals. To find and kill enough food for so many members requires a lot of effort and cooperation. So twice a day the pack rouses itself to action in a frenzy of muzzle licking, chirping, and tail wagging. Then, at a signal from the lead dog, they set off at a fast trot, single file. When a weak, sick, or crippled prey animal is sighted, the wild dogs assume a menacing posture, head down and ears laid back, as they slowly close in on their target. But if their prospective dinner fails to break into a run, the dogs give up and search out another victim. The African wild dog seems unable to give chase unless aroused by a moving target.

Eventually, an antelope or a zebra will panic and take flight, and the wild dogs are after it, full speed. The lead dog always makes the attack, but it is quickly joined by those close behind. Together they finish the kill and begin to eat, often before the dogs in the rear have caught up. No pack member goes hungry, though. Latecomers need only beg, and dogs that have already dined will upchuck meat for them. Food is also offered to the baby-sitters that have remained at the den. In this respect, the African wild dog differs from all other members of the canid family. It doesn't fight over food, but shares what it has, not only with pups and nursing mothers but with any pack member that is hungry.

African wild dogs have long been persecuted by certain people, who view them as evil killers. What is your view?

Does your dog like to chase a moving object?

 The scientific name for the African wild dog is *Lycaon pictus*. It can make its home in dense bush, on the open plains, or in forests, but it has been wiped out of much of its former range and is extremely endangered.

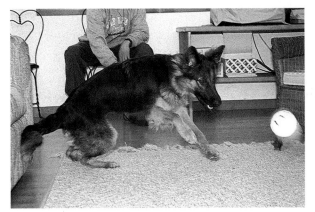

ARCTIC FOX

Imagine living on frozen tundra or on cold ice floes above the Arctic Circle. That's where the Arctic fox makes its home. This prettiest of all wild canids need not worry about competition from any of its cousins. None could survive where temperatures drop below minus 100 degrees Fahrenheit!

The Arctic fox is elegantly designed for life in the far North. The pads of its feet are covered with dense hair to keep them from freezing. Such furry feet also allow this lightweight animal to walk on

 The scientific name for the Arctic fox is *Alopex lagopus*. It lives in the northernmost reaches of North America, Iceland, Greenland, Scandinavia, and Siberia.

snow without sinking in. Its fluffy tail serves as a nose warmer when the animal sleeps. And its long, dense coat, as white as the winter landscape, conceals this little hunter from the birds and lemmings it stalks. Such camouflage also allows the fox to raid polar bear kills, for the nearsighted polar bear can't keep an all-white thief in view.

Summer brings relief to the animals of the Arctic. Along the coastlines, snow recedes and shore birds arrive by the millions to nest. These are easily caught by the Arctic fox, whose winter coat has been replaced by a blue one that matches the coastal rocks. In this season, the Arctic fox gorges and buries food for hard times ahead. Such hoarding is necessary, especially during years when massive numbers of lemmings unaccountably rush into the sea and drown. Then, Arctic foxes go hungry and many die.

Life in the Arctic is not for sissies, and this hard worker is anything but. It is bold, clever, fleet, and curious. In other words, it is a survivor.

Does your dog like to play in the snow?

OTHER WILD COUSINS

Your dog has many wild cousins. In this book you have
met nearly half of them. Here is a list of the others.

Azara's Zorro *Dusicyon gymnocercus*
Bengal Fox *Vulpes bengalensis*
Blanford's Fox *Vulpes cana*
Cape Fox *Vulpes chama*
Corsac Fox *Vulpes corsac*
Crab-Eating Zorro *Cerdocyon thous*
Culpeo *Dusicyon culpaeus*
Golden Jackal *Canis aureus*
Gray Zorro *Dusicyon griseus*
Hoary Zorro *Dusicyon vetulus*
Island Gray Fox *Urocyon littoralis*
Pale Fox *Vulpes pallida*
Raccoon Dog *Nyctereutes procyonoides*
Rüppell's Fox *Vulpes rueppelli*
Sechuran Zorro *Dusicyon sechurae*
Side-Striped Jackal *Canis adustus*
Simien Jackal *Canis simensis*
Small-Eared Zorro *Dusicyon microtis*
Tibetan Fox *Vulpes ferrilata*

GLOSSARY

Canid	a member of the family *Canidae*, which includes dogs and all their wild relatives
Carrion	an already dead animal that is used as food by another animal
Endangered species	a legal term used by the United States government to describe those species that have dropped so low in number that they need special protection
Extinct species	a species of plant or animal that no longer exists in living form
Fahrenheit	a temperature scale that registers freezing at 32 degrees
Foraging	the act of looking for food
Fossil remains	the traces of plants and animals that lived long ago
Gorge	to eat more than can be comfortably digested
Habitat	the special surroundings needed by an animal to make its living and produce young
Hoard	to store food for future use
Ice floes	large, flat, floating ice masses in the Arctic Ocean
Marsupials	a group of animals, living mostly in Australia, in which the female carries her baby in a body pouch
Moat	a ditch filled with water
Muzzle	the jaws and nose of a dog, wolf, fox, or related canid
Prey animals	those animals that serve as food for other animals
Range	the entire geographic area where a particular species is found
Savanna	a flat grassland in a warm climate
Status	the relative standing of an animal in its social group
Tundra	a cold and treeless region in the Arctic where only mosses and low shrubs grow
Whelp	to give birth to a dog, wolf, or related species

INDEX

About the Author

HOPE RYDEN is a naturalist, photographer, and author of seventeen books on wildlife. Her lifelong interest in wild canids prompted her to spend two and a half years in the field, tracking and writing about coyotes. Ms. Ryden's children's books have been named NSTA-CBC (National Science Teachers Association-Children's Book Council) Outstanding Trade Books for Children. She and her husband divide their time between New York City and Wolf Lake, New York.